THE CURSE

The Roxanne Fosch Files 1.5

JINA S. BAZZAR

PREFACE

Yoncey Fosch, the leader of the Unseelie Dhiultadh Clan, would give anything to save his brother from a mysterious plague. Anything, including his leadership mantle and a favor to his deadliest enemy, Queen Titania's consort.

But his actions will have far reaching consequences, and Fosch realizes he is not only unwilling to pay the price, but will defy anyone who calls him on it.

I

THE SECRET

Yoncey Fosch was a cunning man. He was a Fee—or a Dhiultadh—a half one, since his mother had been a notorious Earth witch. He was a man of many qualities, excellent attributes. He was rich, having had centuries of accumulated wealth bestowed upon him by his grandfather, his father, and his late mother. He was ridiculously handsome, having inherited the charms of his pure-blooded father and his beautiful gypsy mother. He had dark hair that brushed soft waves about his shoulders, dark eyes surrounded by thick lashes, giving him a dreamy, romantic look. He had a poet's nose and a sculpted mouth. He was tall, broad, sharp. An undefeatable sword master. Remarkably accurate with a crossbow. The clan's champion with bow and arrow, having won fifty archery competitions in the past two decades. He was a master in martial arts, the head sensei for the scions in his clan. He was even handy with the more modern weapons, though he had no taste for guns.

From his Earth witch mother, he had inherited the ability to power runes, sigils, and glyphs. He learned to control them, to imbue them on living and dead things, to keep them hidden from clever eyes. From his father he learned to hunt, shift, fly, and to rule. His wisdom came from his parents and the long life he'd led. All in all, Yoncey Fosch not only was a blessed being and a product of good genes, but a power to be reckoned with.

He had a younger sister who no one remembered, and whose circumstance had kept him away from, a half-brother and half-sister on his father's side, along with a stepsister from his father's third marriage, and a half-aunt from his mother's side.

He was clan leader of the Unseelie Dhiultadh, where he ruled with an iron fist and a warm heart. He was loved by everyone and everything, including the trees and animals. He was a charismatic man of few words and many wisdoms. But in the spring of 1822, Yoncey Fosch was anything but smart. On the contrary, he was a desperate, grieving man.

He hurried through the Sidhe land, the forbidden land, with a heavy heart and a frantic need. The giant billowing trees rustled and whispered words he didn't care to hear. He had a purpose, a fool's errand. Yes, he was aware of the horrendous mistake he was about to commit. Were his mother alive, he would never need such an atrocious favor.

The animals of this land knew him, recognized a native, though this was no longer his world. Two-headed creatures curiously watched his progress. Rabbit-like hoppers moved along with him, their tails long, reptilian things that helped them jump to the high branches and move through the canopies with ease. His familiar, a young shadow he had fed a traitor once upon a time, stirred, unseen in his higher dimension. Fosch sensed his unease, wanted to reassure his long-time companion, but he was too sick to his stomach, even though he was determined to carry this mission through.

A bird of disproportional size sang a sweet song high above the green, quickly joined by other birds. Fosch barely paid attention, his eyes fixed on the clearing he could make up ahead. It was a secret meeting, a condition both parties had agreed upon. Already, he could make out the silhouette of the man standing in the middle of the clearing, watching some unseen bird or just the beautiful sky. The clearing, a place for peace counseling, was warded against dimensional hops, as safe as the Seelie Castle itself from intruders or direct attacks.

Fosch emerged into the clearing with a sure step, a warrior leader confident of his place, aware that none of the anxiety and turmoil he felt showed through. The sky was a vivid blue bowl, like nothing he had seen in any other world. Had it not been for the grim moment and the high Fee royalty standing with arms crossed a few feet away, Fosch would've stopped to admire the beauty of the sky and land. He was unarmed, also a condition, one he met with honor. He didn't consider Gongo, his familiar, a weapon but a friend. One he knew Oberon was aware of.

Fosch paused four feet away from the Seelie consort. Anything closer would be construed as an insult, and Fosch hadn't asked for this meeting to quarrel.

Oberon raised his arrogant chin. "Fosch."

Fosch returned the chin raise. "Oberon."

Though the Fee royalty looked like an ordinary man of medium size and average stature, Oberon was anything but. A truth that could be gleaned by his straight posture, agility, and the cunning in his deep brown eyes. Or by the sword, for Oberon's swordsmanship was beyond excellent. He was a champion among the best. Fosch had once sparred with him in a duel for the best swordsman, and hours later they had to call it off because both men had duties to attend.

"Let us walk." Oberon turned and moved toward the tree line, hands clasped behind his back.

Fosch stepped beside him, shortening his steps to accommodate Oberon's shorter legs. Both men strolled silently, their faces masks of calm quiet. They looked like two colleagues taking a walk through the woods.

They entered the woods once again, traveled more than a mile through the peaceful, green twilight before emerging atop a sloping hill where the trees ended. Both men regarded the land like the finest of arts. The grass was crisp, crunching underneath their weight. A lonely cloud hung, white and heavy, while the sun shone brightly, cooled by a fragrant breeze.

"Rosalinda passed away last night," Fosch said, words of grief in a land of beauty and serenity. It was almost like blasphemy, to mar the air with words of sadness.

No doubt catching on the note of grief, Oberon tilted his head, focused at a point far in the horizon. "A Clan subject? Merely not just so."

Rosalinda wasn't just a member of the Clan. She was the half-aunt nobody could know, so Fosch merely shrugged. His mission would reveal more than he was comfortable with, anyway.

A two-headed animal darted by, close enough for Oberon to touch. He followed the animal's progress down the hill with his gaze, giving Fosch time to compose his request. He was shorter than Fosch by at least a foot, leaner by at least fifty pounds, but lacked none of the presence or charisma.

"The plague?" Oberon prompted.

Had it been any other Dhiultadh, Oberon would've

walked away, considered his precious time not worth the Dhiultadh's comfort. But Fosch was a man of his word, loyal and honest to a fault, considerate and yet a fearsome ruler, qualities not easily found in such position of power. One or two, perhaps, but not all of them at once, as Oberon had witnessed many rulers who had once been loyal and fair, become corrupted by their position of power. But Fosch had been a leader for many centuries now, and his qualities remained. Had he not been a Dhiultadh, Oberon would've admired him. Moreover, he was an excellent opponent, one Oberon enjoyed. If it weren't for Fosch's heritage, Oberon could've called him a friend. But he was a Dhiultadh, rejected from the Sidhe land, once half-Seelie, half-Unseelie. Or a quarter of each, considering part of him was an Earth witch.

Oberon had grieved over Fosch's mother, Odra, and her tragic death, felt the loss of a good spirit pass by. He had offered his condolences, and his queen's, in person to Fosch.

"Ay, the plague," Fosch grunted.

It was a mysterious disease, its symptoms manifesting gradually, making it hard to identify until it was too late. A shiver, a scratch, a choking cough that cut off as abruptly as it started. A half-hour of extra sleep, an extra glass of water. Then there was the rage. First, just snappish remarks. Then arguments that made no sense. The need to take unnecessary risks. Then the killing spree no one could calm without cutting off the head. So far, Fosch had lost eleven members.

"Gerome," Fosch said.

"Ah. You're sure?" Oberon glanced at Fosch for the first time.

"He slept in yesterday. Snapped mad when I asked about it."

"Ah." Oberon's word carried a world of understanding.

Gerome Archer, Fosch's half-brother.

Both men returned their gazes to the blue sky, contemplating what their short exchange meant in a bigger scheme.

"What is it you want?" Oberon asked.

"The binding stones."

Now Oberon turned to face him. "You wish to banish the plague?"

Fosch shrugged.

He was reaching, but he had to do something. And his year of research had brought forth no fruit.

"The plague is a force, an external one," Fosch said. "My mother has taught me enough to give me a rudimentary understanding of the binding stones." Not a lie, but not the entire truth either. Oberon didn't need to know how much Fosch had been taught. "I will use it in reverse, bind his inner strength to him, banish whatever is left."

Oberon was silent for a few moments. Fosch let him be, aware he'd need to convince him one way or another. He would give anything for a chance to save his younger brother. Torture, a limb, servitude. He'd give his own life for his brothers, particularly Gerome, but his life was something he'd give to a number of people.

"The binding stones may or may not work," Oberon cautioned.

Fosch let out a sigh. "It's the only choice I have. I welcome any suggestions."

"I have none. My people suffer no mortal disease." It was a condescending rebuke, one given without any heat or mockery.

Oberon studied Fosch's face, the strong set of his jaws,

the clear, steady gaze, found no uncertainty, but he hadn't expected any.

"There will be a price, Yoncey Fosch, son of Dhiultadh Bran Fosch. Are you willing to pay?"

Though his stomach jumped in agitated anxiety, Fosch nodded. It went against his better judgment to bargain with a royal Fee, with Queen Titania's consort, no less.

"Then, Dhiultadh Yoncey Fosch, we will meet again in the stone circle, when the sun touches the horizon with gold and red hues."

Both men glanced at the sky, the sun already descending to the other side. Fosch calculated a few hours, at best.

Without a word, both men turned in different directions. Now, Fosch had to go pour over his mother's journals and find the right sigils and runes to use. Perhaps a few glyphs to ground the work. Even though he already had an idea of the ritual he was going to perform, including the herbs and roots he would need, he would go read his mother's journals once more to make sure he didn't miss a step.

By god, he would do this right, no matter what it cost him.

❧ 2 ❧

THE RITUAL

Three days after Fosch acquired the stones, he moved through the gates of his brother's estate in Wyoming. It was located near Yellowstone National Park, five hundred acres of prime land that bordered Idaho on the western side. Archer's home, a sprawling 2,700 square-foot stone building was an L-shaped two-story mansion with eight spacious bedrooms, all luxuriously decorated. There was a pool house where the servants lived, a barn, a chicken coup, a stable with three thoroughbred stallions——one black, one white, and one brown with a honey gold mane. The black one belonged to Archer, the other two to Arianna, Archer's lover.

Fosch would've preferred to have come the previous night, but Gongo had reported that Arianna was home, and so Fosch had to wait. He'd told himself that if Arianna didn't leave by the next night, he'd perform the ritual in front of her, knowing she wouldn't judge him, even if she guessed the length Fosch had taken to procure the stones. After all, she wasn't a Dhiultadh, so she lacked the reservations they had against the Seelie and Unseelie courts. She was, in fact, friendly, if not friends, with the Sidhe land inhabitants. But Arianna had left early this morning and Gongo hadn't seen her come back.

So the house was empty. The servants were back in the pool house, and Laura, the in-house assistant, was asleep in her room on the first floor. The moment Gongo had given the all-clear, Fosch left the clan's compound, fifty thousand acres of prime real estate just outside Bristol, Rhode Island —a forty-five minute travel hopping through the leeway.

Fosch had spent the past three days in his private study, accepting only his house assistant's presence. He had gone over the ritual many times, searching for possible variations and taking notes. Now, here he was. It was late, but he had delayed his arrival on purpose to keep the mission as secretive as possible.

Gongo had gone to the pool house, made sure everyone was deep asleep. He'd been given orders to keep watch. Fosch prowled into the estate like a pro thief, moving from shadow to shadow, through the unlocked front door, up the round staircase, to the second floor. The lamps were still on in his brother's room, but Gongo had never missed a trick, and Fosch slowly opened the heavy door.

The room was masculine, done in dark browns and pale yellows. The heavy furniture and thick antiques, made from dark wood with sharp edges, gleamed with wood polish. The massive fireplace was unlit, clean except for a few logs, ready for use.

Archer was asleep atop the soft duvet, his chest and feet both bare, his golden hair spread over the pillow. One arm was thrown over his face, the other spasmed slightly above his naked stomach. A sheen of sweat covered his brother's torso, even though the windows had been left open and the room was wintry cold despite it being spring.

There was no reason for the sweat, the bare chest, the open window, or the unlit fire. His brother was truly sick, Fosch realized. Until that moment, he had hoped he was wrong, that his brother's snappish mood and the extra sleep had been a reaction to something else. Now, with the truth staring him in the eye, he knew he couldn't fail.

How long did his brother have? How did the plague work, exactly? Why was each individual affected in a different way?

Fosch approached the bed slowly, his steps muffled by the thick winter rugs that covered the gleaming wood planks. An empty glass lay sideways on the stand, a pair of forgotten earrings sat beside it. It was the only feminine touch in the room. For a moment, Fosch stood there, watching the lines on his brother's face. He didn't look peaceful asleep. A half-formed snarl marred his lips, his fingers spasmed, the veins on his neck stood at attention. He looked like a man on the verge of rage.

With a steady hand, Fosch took the prick syringe and injected the horse sedative into Archer's bicep. Archer's arm lowered, his eyes opened a moment, and a growl passed his lips. Then confusion entered his eyes before they glazed, and the snarl died. Archer's arm fell off the bed and Fosch placed it over his naked stomach. Fosch unlaced the small pouch with the herbs and roots he had mashed together, and dipped a small paintbrush into the sharp-smelling concoction.

It took him an hour to draw all the sigils on Archer's chest, abdomen, forehead, and then inlay each sigil with a power rune. He had practiced the precision of the work last night, not wanting to have to draw the symbols more than once and risk smudging the work. The size of the sigil had to be balanced in a way that it could accommodate the smaller runes and binding stones without touching one another.

Fosch placed the exotic binding stones on the middle of each rune, pricked his finger with a sharp scalpel-like talon, and trapped the symbols inside a blood circle. He had to slice his finger a few times to keep on the flow. It was a simple enough task, to trap the energy within the circles, a basic ritual his mother had taught him when he was just a boy.

Next, he circled the sigil on Archer's abdomen, started from the top and moved clockwise. Then moved to the one on the chest, and then forehead, encompassing three of the major seven chakras. Once every sigil had been circled, he placed one more stone, the opposite from the one inside the circle, out of the circle, facing north. Blue for the red stone, green for the yellow, white for the black.

When every symbol had been drawn, bound and powered, Fosch began pulling energy from his body, directing it at the outer stones, which in turn would mirror energy on the inner stones and awaken them. The sigils, healing symbols his mother rarely had to use, would travel through Archer's body, herd whatever unhealthiness lived within, and pull it into the circle. He'd added the containment rune to focus the plague in the middle of the sigil, where each stone would absorb the bad energy, or vibes. He hoped the plague was an ethereal thing, something that wouldn't need to draw blood, as he had read that drawing blood into a healing circle could be as fatal as the disease itself. Considering his only other choice was to let the plague take on its deadly course, he chose to take a chance with the binding stones and the ritual.

Once the inner stone had received enough bad energy, the outer stone would circle around the bloody circle and contain the stone to keep it from overloading and exploding. He had never done this before, and hadn't found the ritual in his mother's journal, his maternal grandmother's, or his great-grandmother's. But there were mentions here and there, a partial containment for the black fever, a healing sigil for the evil snake Fordra—whatever that was —and of course, the binding ritual the Seelie used to banish a treasonous Seelie into their elemental form.

Archer twitched, but otherwise didn't move, and his rhythmic breathing didn't falter. On and on Fosch pulled from his energy, directed it to the binding stones, which in turn awoke the runes, then the sigils, until he began to feel dizzy. He slowed then, knowing if anyone walked in they would find his eyes glowing orange, his hair standing up as if electrocuted, see Archer's bloody, prone body, blood oozing from his nose, ears, eyes, and assume Fosch was performing a ritual attack on his own brother.

Fosch kept pushing energy into the stones until they, too, took on an iridescent glow. It was working. He doubled his efforts, felt the world spin once, braced his legs apart for better balance. When the world spun again, Gongo pressed against his leg and offered some of his energy. Fosch took it, took it all.

For hours, he worked until the center stones floated like mini stars above each rune, and the outer stones orbited around them, never altering from their steady rhythm. Only then did Fosch stop the energy flow. He swayed as he pricked a finger, touched a bloodied tip to the blue glowing stone, and picked it up before it fell back onto his brother's body. The red stone, the middle one, immediately started to fall, and Fosch snatched it before it hit the middle of the rune. There was blood and enough energy for Fosch to realize the plague had been both ethereal and corporal, something he'd have to research later on.

He placed the binding stones, now glowing like colored stars, into the warded pouch Oberon had provided him, and cleaned his brother up. There was nothing he could do about the small wounds left behind from the ritual, but suspicion was a small price his brother would have to pay for good health.

The cleanup took another hour, another sedative, and by then the sky was beginning to clear. He left no traces of his visit behind—no drop of blood, no symbols, no scents but that of ozone, and the small dash-like wounds he knew Archer would always wonder about, even after he could no longer see them.

When a fresh wave of dizziness made Fosch stop and brace a hand on the wall to balance himself, he conceded that perhaps he should've confessed his plans to Arianna, considering she, too, could power the runes. Better than him, since she didn't need to pull energy from herself, but could manipulate lost energy as well, pulling it from the environment into herself, a work in progress, or redirect it to wherever she wished. She was a being of energy, from a planet billions of light years away, and Fosch was glad there were only two others like her. They were dangerous beings, capable of killing entire planets, as they had done once when they fell through the portal. But despite all of Arianna's faults, she was loyal, willing to die for those she loved, and Fosch sometimes suspected that Archer might be one of them.

Other times, he pitied Archer for his love. Because as an outsider to the drama, Fosch understood Archer and Arianna would never mate, given they weren't equals. Although Archer was no weakling, she was stronger than him by leagues. Indeed, Archer was a formidable man— strong, capable, fair, and just. He was one of a few who Fosch admired, respected, called an equal. It was why the knowledge of the plague infecting him hit Fosch the hardest.

Gongo pressed against Fosch's leg, still invisible, and Fosch, sensing his worry and anxiety, sent him a reassuring thought.

"Nothing a good sleep won't cure," he told his faithful friend, and pushed himself from the wall.

3

THE BARGAIN

It took Fosch a few months and about a dozen other rituals before he had purged the cursed plague from his clan. It had come to be known that those who escaped the plague awoke in the morning exhausted and with three strange scars, or swore that an angel with huge feathery wings came to their windows at night and stared at them until they had been cured.

Only three members had died, and only because they had been too stubborn to report the symptoms, making it too late to save them. Fosch had performed the mercy kills himself. He grieved for those three, but such was life.

There were those who lived too far for him to reach in time. He couldn't hop the leeway over the ocean, and ships took too long to cross. There was also the outbreak in Siberia, where the plague had killed eight members of the clan, something that Fosch had only heard about a few months later. He had grieved for those, too. The Belochkin family had been a close acquaintance, but their deaths happened before he had acquired the binding stones.

The clan was too big and too spread out, Fosch had

often told the high council. They needed to split, form sub-clans that responded to their leader. However, he had always been out-voted. It was only now, whenever he performed the mercy kills, he hated he had been the one to suggest they vote for each major change.

Fosch kept the stones for an entire year after he'd done the last ritual, before returning them to Oberon. Though he had no doubt the plague was over, if any of the members exhibited signs of the plague, it had been agreed that Oberon would return the binding stones to Fosch without any further demands.

"What does completion of the bargain entail?" Fosch asked Oberon, standing on the same spot as when they'd met two years ago.

The sky was still that vivid blue, the trees still lush and full, whispering rustling breezes behind them like the soothing caress of a beloved. The ground was as green as it could possibly be, full of insects and unseen miniature life.

Oberon jiggled the pouch, making the stones emit an appealing sound. He took his time replying, though he'd had two years to contemplate his asking price. The knots in Fosch's stomach grew tighter, but his face remained passive. He had already taken steps to ensure the safety of the clan by renouncing his leadership and making sure word trav-elled and reached far into the Sidhe land.

"Completion of the bargain… perhaps an offspring would be a fitting price." Oberon mused.

Fosch's stomach contents curdled.

"A Dhiultadh, one strong enough to power the binding stones and still live to tell. It makes me wonder what an offspring of yours and a Seelie would create."

Fosch hadn't expected such a request, so he hadn't rehearsed a convincing argument against it. A mistake, as he was well-aware of the difficulties the Sidhe faced to produce offspring.

His offspring would already have some Fee blood, and a couple, maybe three generations later, that scion would be pure-blooded enough to mate and produce one or two Seelie before infertility kicked in. A matter of fifty years, perhaps, and a few new Sidhe pure bloods would be born. And Fosch would be helping his enemy's army grow. His clan would never forgive him.

"No Seelie would accept a coupling with a Dhiultadh," Fosch said. "Much less an Unseelie Dhiultadh."

"Nay, we would not. For that, you will produce an offspring that will be raised according to our rules and traditions here in the Seelie land."

Fosch tightened his jaws and balled his fists. "It is increasingly hard to produce an offspring. Surely, your highness, you know this." For the Unseelie Dhiultadh, although blessed once with fertility, now face difficulties to reproduce as well.

Oberon grunted. "You Dhiultadh are increasingly stubborn. Your better peers haven't had such difficulties, for they are flexible creatures."

Once, a long time ago, Verenastra, Titania's daughter, met Madoc, the leader of the Unseelie court, and produced with him an offspring, a daughter she named Oonagh. Fosch's clan members were descendants of Oonagh and Finvarra, the bastard son of the current ruler of the Unseelie court, Queen Maive. When Madoc tried to kill Verenastra, she fled the Sidhe land and mated Elvilachious, the leader of the Tristan star. They bred and started a different line altogether, now called the Seelie Dhiultadh, or the Unseelie Dhiultadh's *better kin*.

"Their blood is diluted," Fosch argued without heat.

He had never been one to consider his cousin clan

weaklings the way all the elders from his clan suggested. And once, during his father's reign, he had dared to voice his opinion and almost gotten himself ostracized for it. After that particular incident had been straightened, Fosch stopped voicing his opinion, even when a debate arose, and they often did, and some of the elders aimed daring looks at him.

Yes, his mother had not been a Dhiultadh, but his parent's marriage had been an unconventional arrangement, a way to strengthen the clan during a time of war, and even that hadn't worked well. Fosch, the firstborn, was supposed to be a scion of the Earth Witch Coven, but his father, the clan leader at that time, had circumvented the agreement by declaring Fosch the next clan leader, subjecting Fosch's first century to a rigorous life in training, making Fosch unfit for the Earth Witch Clan.

A long, bloody feud had followed his father's declaration, until his mother had produced Cora, a sister Fosch had met only a handful of times, and who now ruled over the dwindling coven. His parents were the only permitted interspecies marriage, and not a single member of the clan protested when his ancestors—arrogant, backward leaders of the clan—had decided that any interspecies marital relations would dilute their blood, and decreed such thing a blasphemy. Of course at the time of this decree, breeding hadn't been an issue, but a blessing. A lot of his ancestors had more than a half-dozen siblings. Some even more than a dozen.

His cousin clan, the Seelie Dhiultadh, on the other hand, bred more easily because of their flexibility and willingness to explore interspecies relationship, and even with this truth facing them like a bright star, the clan still refused to expand. Fosch suspected that one day the clan would see reason, or be forced to, when the Unseelie Dhiultadh number begin to dwindle into extinction.

Oberon waved a hand dismissively before placing his hands behind his back.

"We talk not of the Tristan clan. An offspring is my bargaining price, Yoncey Fosch, son of Dhiultadh Bran Fosch."

Fosch inclined his head in agreement, though his insides screamed in denial.

"But I will ease the burden for you," Oberon said. "I want a half-human scion, to breed four royals for my queen."

Astonished, Fosch turned to him. "For you? An offspring of mine and a human for you?"

Oberon tilted his head up, his brown eyes sharp. "It offends you."

Fosch shrugged. Fulfilling his side of the bargain didn't mean he had to like it.

Though both his stance and Fosch's were relaxed, tense energy crackled around them.

Oberon returned his gaze to the land. "To answer your question, not for me, nay. But I will let you know that the third generation of this offspring will be Seelie enough for my queen."

Ah. A human hybrid, easy enough to produce. It would already be part Fee. And it would produce four offspring's. Each would mate and produce as many as they were able, increasing the Sidhe genes. Those would produce as many as they could, and once Queen Titania deemed them Seelie enough, she would choose the ones that showed promise and pair them with her best. The Seelie army would grow. God knew by how many.

"For how long?" Fosch asked.

"The scion will be born and raised at court. You are

allowed to visit and be presented as the sire, if you so wish. Once the four offspring are produced, the scion can leave with you or return to the mortal realm."

Fosch was quiet for a long time, contemplating the asking price for his brother's life, along with a dozen others. He didn't regret his deed, the bargain, or even the asking price. No, what stuck in his craw was the human part. He didn't like humans, never made it a secret. Could even be why Oberon specified the human hybrid. Fosch wouldn't have any trouble handing over the scion. He wouldn't want to present himself as the sire. A human hybrid—nothing but an abomination. Not even his cousin clan stooped so low as to breed with a human.

To reproduce four times, it would have to be female, so any male offspring would be disregarded. What a clever asking price. It was true that the difficulties to breed extended as far as their avoidance to mate outside the clan. But a human hybrid was easy to come by. In fact, it would be more troublesome to procure a worthy human to carry on his seed.

"I will need to find a suitable vessel for my seed," Fosch said.

Oberon inclined his head and walked away.

Fosch hoped his first offspring was female so he wouldn't need to produce more than one, and that this female would produce four male offspring so Oberon wouldn't be able to breed an army out of them.

In any case, what was he supposed to do with a human hybrid after that? The clan would have no use for it. They would make that scion's life a misery of ridicule and humiliation.

Fosch paused in the forest, his head cocked as if listening to some inner thought. Gongo appeared by his side, still the size of a child even though he was 356 years old. Fosch met the understanding in the shell-shaped eyes of his companion.

"We never agreed upon a timeline," he said to his familiar, who crouched beside him.

"No, master," it hissed in a deep tone.

Fosch laughed then, a long booming sound that echoed and spooked the exotic birds into flight.

❧ 4 ☙

THE AWARENESS

EARLY 2014

Arianna Lenard stumbled on a rock, blind with grief and rage. The daughter of her womb, the son of her heart, and the friend to her soul, all gone within the span of a week. The first, murdered. The second, no more than a vegetable. The third… missing. Arianna had come to the Low Lands to seek revenge, but revenge wasn't what she got.

She stumbled again, fell to her knees.

"You could always join me," said a nasal rumble behind her.

"Never," she spat through gritted teeth.

The man sighed, dramatically. "There will be only two sides to stand when this is over, Ari. Either you're with me or against."

"I'd rather die a permanent death," she hissed, clutching the needle pointed rocks hard enough for the skin of her hands to break.

Blood welled, but the sharp pain kept her focused.

"We cannot stop it," the man said. "Even if you kill me over and over, the inevitable will happen as nature wills it to. This way, I ensure control and authority over it all."

"And who made you a god?" Arianna sneered.

She had never used such a condescending tone, not even to Remo, but she felt detached from the person she'd been a week ago.

"You are nothing but another creature," she said. "Just another one of them. Soon they'll wonder why it's you and not someone else. What do you think will happen then?"

Remo said nothing.

Arianna threw her arms wide. "Look what the three of us did. Take a look around."

They both looked at the complete destruction their arrival had caused over half a millennium ago. Though neither of them remembered how the land used to be, both had seen enough of paintings and portraits to know they had destroyed one of the most beautiful planets in existence. Nothing had escaped the Quasar Stellar Beings arrival—no insect, no plant or tree, no animal, not even the warriors sent to fight for the land.

"They're coming, Ari, with or without your approval," Remo said calmly.

Arianna stood slowly, her bedraggled appearance a warped mirror of her grief.

"I will find a way to stop it. I'll shove you through that portal, then close that thing behind you."

Her soft green eyes blazed with determination, but Remo only watched her patiently. Once, he had been as tall and beautiful as she, but power and greed had corrupted him into this… this manifestation.

"Look at you, Re. You're losing yourself to it. It has transformed you into a monster."

He smirked, raising his arms. "Power is a wonderful thing, Ari. External appearance means nothing."

He let go of the glamor he held always in check, and a blast of energy hit Arianna so hard she took a reflexive step back.

She hissed at his knowing smugness. "You have been feeding… from what? Who?"

A long time ago, she had hunted with him, revved in the energy they could cultivate from a being. But that was before, when she didn't know she had to hurt someone or something to make power. Both she and Zantry had recoiled from that notion and stopped draining things, took only enough to survive. And only from a source of water. For a time then, Remo had joined them, had been content with what they got. Once, she had even considered him a friend, a mirror to her soul.

Remo came closer, pulled the corrupt energy back into himself. "You said it yourself. Look around you, Ari, see what three of us have done. The portal can't be closed. What do you think will happen when they come pouring in, unchecked?"

"You killed Cara, my own daughter," Arianna choked.

Remo cocked his head, his beady eyes flat as he contemplated her. "You created her to kill me first."

His words felt like an icy blow, made more potent by the truth in them. She had made Cara to kill Remo, being that she was half-Dhiultadh and half of Arianna's womb. She had learned long ago that both powers combined could freeze a portal, and that mingled into one, they could destroy it. Now she would never know, for her daughter was dead. Logan, Cara's mate, took her loss so hard he had retreated deep into himself, nothing more than a vegetable now, unwilling to even raise a spoon to his mouth.

Arianna had always known the danger she was

thrusting her daughter into, but she had never imagined throwing her to Remo Drammen alone or unprepared.

She whirled around before she did something she'd regret later. Killing him would be satisfying, even if he'd return after a few weeks, but if he was telling the truth, which he had proven he was, then the portal could activate at a time when Remo wasn't present and other creatures of the Quasar Stellar would start pouring in, unchecked. The land here was already dead, and it was possible that nothing would happen. But if the creatures learned to travel through the paths, like Arianna, Remo, and Zantry had learned… and the three of them had destroyed an entire planet to physically manifest… Arianna didn't want to think about the consequences if Remo wasn't present to guard the portal, to bind whatever came through.

Furious with herself and the sense of futility, Arianna balled her fists and began marching away, searching the path in the ether she had once marked for emergencies.

"And Zantry?" She paused. "What did you do to him?"

When only silence met her, she flashed to Earth, to the only person she knew would give her the space and solace she needed.

❧ 5 ❧

THE GRIEVING

A rianna fell into the middle of her friend's living room in Brooklyn, on the middle of a glyph that had been carved into the mortar during the building of the two-story home.

Matilda spilled the mouthful she had just sipped onto herself and jumped to check on her friend. She wasn't surprised with the sudden appearance, no, she had been expecting her friend to arrive ever since she'd heard the dreadful news. Although, Matilda thought she would be arriving in a more conventional way.

She hid the shock that jolted through her at Arianna's unkempt appearance—the torn and bloodied clothes, hair wild and loose, knotted and greasy. Matilda touched a tentative hand to her friend's shoulder, unsure if the blood on her clothes was her own. She felt the tremors that shook Arianna's shoulders first, heard the sobs next. Her heart went out to her friend, hurt for her, for the horrific loss she had endured this past week. She understood tears didn't come easily to Arianna, so she crouched beside her, gathered the grieving woman to her chest, met her husband's gaze before he stood and left the room.

When Arianna was spent, Matilda helped her to stand, then led her to the spare bedroom on the second floor. Without a word, she helped Arianna undress, cataloguing her injured palms, raw knees, before helping her to the bathroom and under the hot spray.

When Arianna emerged, clean and naked from the bathroom a few minutes later, she found soft pajamas folded atop the single bed, dressed mechanically. She hadn't cried before, hadn't shed a tear even when she'd learned her world was turning upside down, upended in a way that dropped away all she had cherished and nurtured. But the hopelessness of today, of realizing she couldn't take her revenge on her foe for the murder of her daughter without dooming the entire universe, broke a fundamental piece of herself. She wished for Zantry, the only friend who could understand, but he had also mysteriously disappeared. She believed Remo was responsible for that too, but his lack of gloating over his victory had yet to worry her. She believed Zan would show up soon, as he always came back, and together they would figure something out.

Matilda brought her chamomile tea and sat with her in companionable silence as Arianna drank it all, knowing the charmer had used a soothing spell in the tea. When she was done, Matilda picked a hair brush from the nightstand and gently brushed Arianna's glossy black hair. Then she braided it down her back. Tucked her in.

Woke her up for dinner. Watched helplessly as her friend retreated deeper and deeper into herself.

For months, Arianna stayed with Matilda and her husband, tucked inside her own world, in a guest room in a town house in Brooklyn. Rarely did she come out to the living room or speak. She asked only about her friend Zan, but Matilda was sorry that she hadn't heard anything new. He hadn't returned, and the Hunters were beginning to lose hope.

Every now and again, Archer would call to ask if Matilda had any news about Arianna or Zantry, and he would hang up the moment he heard the negative reply. Matilda informed Arianna about the calls, of course, but she seemed to not care the world believed her dead.

Exactly one year after Arianna flashed into Matilda's living room, she came out of her bedroom, dressed in the jeans and green blouse Matilda had bought her a few months back. She moved into the living room, her posture straight, eyes determined.

She looked well, though far from recovered. Matilda had offered counseling, meditation, even crafted a few charms to dull the edge of Arianna's grief. The charms lay forgotten inside the stand drawer beside the single bed Arianna had occupied for the past year, and the meditations and counseling only went as far as she was willing to let it go. Matilda understood more than the death of her daughter was bothering her friend. More than her daughter's mate's withdrawal. More than Zantry's disappearance.

"You're leaving," Matilda said.

"It's time," Arianna said. "We'll talk about all this soon, Matilda."

They ate breakfast in silence, and when Arianna stood to leave, Matilda walked her to the door.

"You will come again, Ari. Choose wisely. Consider your own sake."

Arianna held Matilda's gaze, then softened and hugged her friend.

"I'll do what's necessary. I will come back before anything is decided."

Arianna left, took a cab to West 79th, and headed straight to Belvedere Castle, where she knew, ironically enough, was a straight path to the Sidhe land that didn't intersect with the Low Lands, as she didn't want to give Remo any inkling of her whereabouts.

She was welcomed warmly by the Seelie courtiers and led to Leon, Enforcer of the Seelie Court. Leon, Titania's right-hand and confidant, led Arianna directly into Queen Titania's inner sanctum without even announcing her presence. She knelt in front of her queen and bowed her head. Arianna, still standing, only lowered her head in a deferent bow, for Queen Titania wasn't her queen. And when she raised her head, she met Titania's eyes without fear of retribution.

"Arianna Lenard," Queen Titania said. "Where is your other half?"

"Dead."

Everyone turned their heads to gape at her, eyes wide.

Queen Titania straightened and waved a hand at the royal courtiers gathered around the room. At once, everyone began to exit, muttering under their breaths.

Arianna ignored the whispered words and held Queen Titania's gaze without flinching. It was time. She had waited long enough for Zantry. He should've come back within weeks of his disappearance. But he hadn't, and she'd waited for an entire year.

Only one thing would've prevented Zantry from coming back—true death.

❧ 6 ❧

THE PLAN

Arianna was given a royal suite, a celebration, and a dinner in her honor. She dressed in the Seelie finery she was provided, ate, drank, and danced. But her mind was somewhere else, her heart frozen somewhere deep. She would've rather hurried things along, but after she explained the situation to Queen Titania, the plan and their part in it, they received a message from Queen Maeve, requesting audience and permission to talk to Arianna.

Arianna had gotten delayed, and there was nothing she could do but wait for the Unseelie convoy to arrive the next day. She pretended she was normal, attending both festivities thrown in her name, deflected the flirtatious attempts of the Seelie males, and danced another night with Oberon.

But the third day finally came, and with it, Queen Maeve and her royal entourage. It took Arianna time and effort to convince both queens. There were lots of arguments and denials on both parts before she was able to make them see reason. There was no other way, they had no other choice but to follow her plan.

She was forced to reveal a few secrets, explain what she had learned before she'd retreated to wait for her friend Zantry. She made the queens understand that they would had to work, if not together, then in tandem with each other. The queens had a lot to lose by arguing, and fools they were not, so they listened attentively, even if they recoiled from her plan.

A fortnight later, everything was ready. Now, all Arianna had to do was to convince her friend Matilda to perform the ritual.

Matilda and her husband sat on the couch together and listened to Arianna explain her plan with precision, proving to them that although she'd been idle during her stay, her mind hadn't. The entire plan hinged on her friend's acceptance of the unspeakable, so once Arianna was finished, she got up to give the couple some alone time to debate among themselves.

When she returned, Matilda was standing at the window, watching the New York traffic, her husband nowhere to be found.

"Do you know what you ask of me, Arianna?" Matilda didn't look back at her.

"Yes."

Matilda would be considered a practitioner of dark arts, would even be banned from the local coven. The residual of the dark ritual would reflect upon every work she performed after that.

"Have you talked to Archer?"

"No."

"Are you going to?" Matilda turned to look at her friend.

Arianna met her eyes with a steady gaze. None of the grief and pain she had left with two weeks ago showed through.

"No. You will tell him you have no news of me, as you have been doing for the past year."

Matilda sighed and moved to stand beside Arianna, took her friend's hand into her dark ones.

"Can't you find another way?"

"I have tried. There's no other option."

"If I do what you ask of me..." Matilda took a deep breath, "you understand that you'll be human. You will lose what is essentially you."

Arianna's soft green eyes held no fear, no doubt. "I know."

"You might forget about everyone, everything. I don't know if I can spare that part."

"I understand."

"How are you going to teach the child if you can't remember? If you don't have any more magic?"

"I won't."

"You..." Matilda dropped Arianna's hand and huffed a humorless laugh. "You want to forget, don't you? You think that if I do this, the pain will go away, that you will no longer grieve?"

Arianna said nothing.

Matilda turned around and moved away a few steps, then whirled back, her brown eyes blazing with anger.

"What about those of us you'll leave behind? Don't we get to grieve, to feel?"

"If we don't do this, it won't matter who can grieve or not, Mattie. The portal can't be closed. If we kill Remo, even for a few weeks, the portal could activate at a time he isn't present to capture the beings. I'm giving you a chance here to close the portal and get rid of Remo." Arianna splayed her hands. "I can't do this again and know I'll lose what I cherish in the end, Mattie. This way, I give you all I have, without feeling the pain."

"And get a chance to live a normal life, away from everyone."

"Do you begrudge me that wish, Mattie?"

"And if it doesn't work? Then we lose you for nothing?"

"It will work. I have both the Sidhe queens invested on the plan."

"Both? Seelie and Unseelie? You bargained with them?"

"Not bargained, no. I explained the situation, told them I could give them a weapon to fight the invasion. They're both willing to teach it all it'll need, mentally, physically, magically. It's the best weapon I can make. The best plan—"

"It's a baby!" Matilda exploded. "It's a life, for god's sake, not a weapon!"

Arianna's eyes iced over, her voice turned frigid. "It's a deadly weapon that will be created for this sole purpose. It will be raised and trained by both Sidhe queens to save all those planets. At the end, it too will die to protect you all. Don't belittle it."

Matilda swallowed a terse reply, aware she hit a festering wound. "What about Archer?"

"He already thinks I'm dead. He's already grieved for me. I am not his mate, Matilda. He'll find someone, eventually."

Matilda closed her eyes, grief beginning to carve a hole inside her.

"And if I do it wrong?"

"You won't."

"Maybe if I leave something for you to build on, you won't have to forget. To… to… maybe like with Cara, maybe I don't have to dabble in the dark power. I can invert some of your energy inward and we can work something from there."

They had already tried that before. Furthermore, Arianna didn't want to raise a child or be part of that child's life, knowing she would be sacrificing it later. That knowledge had killed her daughter, had kept her from teaching Cara the hardest of the weaves, from pushing her hard enough. She'd been soft with Cara because she had cared. She didn't have the heart to do it all over again and do it right.

Matilda exhaled. "It'll take time pulling everything inward, getting it ready."

"As much as it needs."

"It could be years," she exaggerated. "It's not like I can yank it all and redirect it toward your womb."

Arianna inclined her head in agreement.

"Won't you want to know how it ends?" Matilda snapped.

Arianna shrugged. The truth was, she felt empty. "It'll be a means to the end, nothing else. Fitting, don't you think, for the trio to undo themselves?"

"Zantry might still come back."

"No. He could've come back within a few days. A few weeks, at most. It's been more than a year, Mattie. He doesn't register in the Ether, and hasn't for this entire year. I know something bad happened to him. Remo knows it, so it must've been him."

"Maybe…"

Arianna shook her head. "Not without letting me know."

Matilda slumped to the sofa, closing her eyes in defeat. She understood the necessity of her friend's sacrifice, but damn it, Arianna was the closest thing she had for a sister.

"When?" Matilda asked.

"Tonight." Arianna sat beside her. "We'll start with the ritual tonight."

"And once you're ready to go? How'll we know?"

"I'll be watched by the Sidhe at all times. No one is to interfere until I've conceived."

"Do you have the father ready?"

"No. But you'll make me want to be near someone strong and capable. The Sidhe will make sure it's someone compatible for the task ahead."

"And once the baby's born?"

"The Seelie will come for you. You'll erase my memory, give me an impression of a past again, then let me be. You can even show up later on, introduce yourself." Arianna gave a faint smile.

But they both knew that wouldn't happen. Once the dark ritual was over, they would never see each other again.

7

THE SECOND CHANCE
PRESENT DAY: 2018

Fosch picked flowers on his way home, soft pink roses entwined with wild blue lilies. In his other hand he had a box of chocolate, along with a bag of Italian takeout from the restaurant on the corner. He was happy, free, in love.

"Witchy witch," he called the moment he opened the front door.

"Here."

Fosch followed the voice to the kitchen, where the woman he had fallen in love with sat, rubbing a small bump over her belly. Her aura flickered with magic, fainter than last week's, but he kept his concern hidden.

"I brought you chocolate." He placed the Godiva box in front of her on the table.

She sniffed and curved her lips into a smile. "And Italian. Alfredo sauce."

Fosch chuckled. "And flowers. For my lovely witch."

But Bella didn't reach for either, just continued to rub the bump over her belly in slow circles. Fosch's focus sharpened on the movement, on the pallor of her face, the feel of her aura. She was hurting.

"What is it?" he asked.

"I guess I'm just restless." She gave a faint smile.

He brushed her hair back from her face, noticing the sweat along her hairline.

"You sure?" he asked, guessing the temperature in the house to be below seventy again. "Want me to make you some tea?"

"Nah, just finished a cup." She waved at the empty cup on the sink, and stood slowly, the effort taking more care than it warranted. She smiled at Fosch. "Can we eat later? I'd like to watch a movie first."

"Sure." He took her clammy hand in his and led her to the sofa.

He would've rather carried her, but knew pride wouldn't permit Bella to accept it. So he got ready to catch her should she fall, and she indeed looked ready to drop. He fussed over the pillows, arranging them so she would be comfortable, then pulled her legs up to rest over his knees and began massaging one foot, then the other. She was asleep within minutes.

He watched her sleep for a long time, touched her knee, her hand, brushed the bump over her belly, careful not to wake her. Worry tightened his gut. She was only twenty weeks along and the pregnancy was already draining her. Sometimes he cursed himself for being a fool, for being selfish for wanting this. He hadn't forgotten about his bargain with Oberon, but Bella wasn't human, thus the bargain couldn't hold true.

Fosch glanced at the faint flicker in her aura and frowned at it. It had gotten fainter as the pregnancy progressed, and it worried him that should it continue to weaken, it might look plain and human by the time she gave birth. And unless her aura did a quick turnaround, he would have a lot to explain. To his clan, to Oberon.

Of course, he could continue to keep Bella and the pregnancy a secret until she was well and her aura regained the witchy sheen. He hated the lies, the need to evade his brother's questions, the secretive life he was leading. He was glad he no longer had any responsibilities to the clan, having shrugged off the leadership mantle the week following his brother's healing ritual, to ensure Oberon couldn't take advantage of Fosch's position. He'd played with exposure a few times, just to ensure that he no longer was worthy of the position, acting reckless and adventurous to keep the clan and his brother from suspecting any alternative reason for his sudden change of character. He had made himself an intermediary between the human government and the clan so he could never again assume the role of leader. And he had never regretted it.

There had been challenges issued to Archer over the leadership, as there should've been, and Fosch had counseled and attended them all, giving his younger brother all his support, helping him fit and mold the mantle onto his shoulders.

Now, almost two centuries later, Fosch had never felt happier for his renegade status. He glanced down at the faint flickering of Bella's aura, the small lump over her belly. The child wouldn't be a pure blooded Dhiultadh, but then, neither was he, even if his mixed status had made him stronger than a pure blood. And his child would be strong, of that he would make sure of. A child he'd be proud to teach what his parents had taught him. The fact that Bella was a witch—albeit a watered down one— meant the scion would also be able to power runes, hopefully manipulate energy as well, instead of merely being able to identify them.

Fosch felt a frisson of adrenaline and couldn't wait to start teaching his son, or daughter, the art of magic. Would the scion be able to shift? Probably, since the alternative form was a dominant trait, even weakened as it would be. Closing his eyes, he leaned back on the sofa and dreamt of a future.

Bella dreamt of Mattie again. The black woman was familiar, though Bella had only met her in dreams. Mattie beckoned, but she didn't follow. She knew where the dream would lead her. She'd had this dream over and over. Once or twice before she had conceived, and often after. These days, she might dream of her twice in the same day.

Like most times, Bella was in a strange, yet familiar forest, the trees tall, the animals strange. Here in the dream, she recognized the land, knew it was the Sidhe land. Mattie called, and when Bella glanced up she was looking into a mirror, but the woman who looked back was different. She had long, straight black hair that shimmered in the moonlight, soft green eyes that gleamed with intelligence and power. In the dream, Bella knew this woman was her reflection, but Bella's hair was short and dark brown, her eyes more hazel than green. There was a resemblance, yes, but again, the woman in the mirror wasn't her. She had a leaner face, her body thinner. They were both tall, had similar light complexions, high cheekbones. Bella always had a twinge of grief when looking into the eyes in the mirror, shared with the reflection the acute despair eating her from inside.

Mattie called again, and like in the way of dreams, the

mirror disappeared and she was now standing in the Seelie court, facing Queen Titania and her royal entourage. Queen Maeve entered the room from a doorway to her left, moving regally to stand beside Queen Titania. The courtiers knelt and bowed to both queens, Seelie and Unseelie alike, but Bella did neither.

A royal Fee, a Seelie, whom Bella recognized in the dream to be Oberon, detached from the group and approached her, radiating sadness, even if his eyes remained flat. He knelt in front of her as he took her cold hand in his.

"M'lady."

She already knew what was to come, so she braced herself.

Something brushed against her cheek, and jolting, Bella awoke, still on the sofa, the face of the man she loved above hers, his eyes concerned.

"I fell asleep," she said, apologetically.

"Bad dream?" He brushed a knuckle over her pale cheek.

Another one. He tried to stifle his concern. She needed a healer, but not a human one. Where could he take her and still keep her a secret?

8

THE VIGIL

On the other side of the street, Oberon watched the exchange, unseen under a heavy glamour. He knew this chain of event would be problematic, even if he had refused to interfere. But it struck him then and there, while he kept watch over Bella, that perhaps this was meant to be all along. Now, he waited. If the dark witch was right, at the end of the next trimester, Oberon would be taking Bella and the offspring to the Seelie land with him.

Despite Leon's doubts and his advisor's arguments, Oberon wasn't one to question fate. He might've been wary when Fosch and Bella had met, by chance, soon after the dark witch had completed the ritual, but Oberon couldn't have asked for a better turn of events. He had contemplated snatching Bella the moment she'd conceived, as had been arranged with Arianna. But it would be to him Fosch would come first, and the dark witch had reassured him by the end of the trimester the residual of the ritual would be sucked inward, a last layer of protection for the scion.

Against protests, he had left Bella to her own devices, to live as much of the mortal's life as she had wanted to. The remnants of the dark witch's ritual was fading as promised, and soon Oberon would be able to claim his prize from Fosch and fulfill his agreement with Arianna.

Oberon watched as Fosch rubbed Bella's foot, brushed his hand over her belly. If he hadn't known any better, Oberon would've guessed Fosch was in love, or drunk.

Oberon chuckled and shook his head. Fate, that mysterious force.

It complicated things, yes. He understood his advisor's warnings, but this scion was so much more than what they'd expected. He understood there would be need of treachery, of treaded steps to acquire this particular scion, to return Bella to the Seelie land for protection until the Sidhe healers could find a way to make her recover. No, this hadn't been part of their agreement with Arianna, but Queen Titania and Maeve had decided upon it and sent inquiries over their lands.

He frowned into the night, knowing that this part would be trickier.

"Do you believe, Leon, that Zantry is no longer?" Oberon asked.

His enforcer contemplated his question. "It has been a long time since his disappearance. I can't say."

"Perhaps, if he happened to return, then Arianna wouldn't be so inclined to stay human."

Leon angled her head, looking at the couple on the sofa. She'd been a fierce advocate against the couple and had predicted a gruesome feud between the court and the Dhiultadh.

"Arianna claimed he hadn't registered for more than a full cycle," Leon said. "She wouldn't make such claim lightly." She turned to face her liege. "We have found another patch of death in the Belogia Belt. Remo is at it again."

❧ 9 ❧

THE PAYOFF

The moment Bella entered her third trimester, Fosch knew. The flicker was barely present then, gone entirely for days. The pregnancy hadn't been kind on her and it tore him apart to watch her wasting away, little by little. He had contemplated getting rid of it, and even danced around the topic, testing the waters to see how Bella would react. But the possibility of losing that scion had put such despair in her eyes Fosch put the topic aside without broaching it.

She was thirty-five weeks along when Oberon came. By then, Bella's aura had become plain blue, completely human. There was nowhere to hide, and he was ashamed to admit to himself he had considered that coward's path plenty of time during the past weeks. But because of the bargain, Oberon would be able to find him wherever he went, and he couldn't leave Bella alone, now that she tired merely by standing up too long.

He had taken her to a shaman far in the wilderness of Prague, a witch in the deserts of Egypt, and a human healer. All concurred the scion was fine and in good health, and all were confused when Fosch explained the aura angle.

There was nothing to do but wait and pray that Oberon wouldn't show.

But show he did, one afternoon when Bella was taking a nap before they had to go see the human healer again. Fosch stepped aside for Oberon to enter. There was no need for pretense. If Oberon was here in such a time, it was because he knew. So he invited Queen Titania's consort into his home and offered him hospitality, per the Sidhe code. Oberon moved to the window on the far side of the comfortable living room, glanced out at the spot where he usually watched Bella from, before turning to face Fosch.

"You have met the bargain, Dhiultadh Yoncey Fosch. I have come to collect."

The room flashed in Fosch's mind. Although he had been expecting it, Oberon's words were like a hard blow to his heart. He wanted to howl in protest, to shout the injustice of the world to the universe. Instead, he crossed his arms over his chest and tilted his head, his expression mocking, arrogant.

"As I recall it," Fosch said, "our bargain entailed a human hybrid, did it not?"

"Indeed."

"Then the bargain has not been met yet."

Oberon raised his head, listening to Bella's soft breathing. "Is she not carrying yours?"

Fosch's stomach muscles cramped. "She is. But she's not human."

Oberon watched him with cold brown eyes, said nothing.

Bella hadn't been human when they met, but she was very much human now. He had a wild thought that perhaps Oberon could see the future, or had been told about Bella before the bargain had been struck. But no Seelie or Unseelie could see the future, not even in glimpses.

"Bella is a descendant of a witch line," Fosch said. "Her human-looking aura is only due to the weakening effect the scion has upon her."

"Ay? It was made known to me that when a female carries a scion she becomes stronger, resonating both life forces."

Fosch inclined his head. It was true, and he had often wondered about it.

"You can verify her heritage for yourself," he said. "She is an offspring of an air witch and a water mage."

"Who?" Oberon asked.

He hadn't heard the details of the charmer's ritual, hadn't wanted to know. Too much darkness and sorcery, he had argued, as had both queens. But Arianna had been determined to go through with it even without the Sidhe's approval, and Queen Titania had at last conceded to take in the scion and prepare it, as Arianna had instructed.

"Who?" Fosch repeated. "Her mother died when she was but a child. Her father was killed during the mage war ten years ago."

Fosch thought he caught a flash of surprise in Oberon's eyes and he pressed.

"And there's still a chance that the scion is male," A slim one according to the ultrasound, but slim was better than nothing. "And once the scion is born, Bella's aura will return to normal. Borrenski said this can happen, that sometimes the scion takes a lot from the mother." He knew he sounded desperate, so he forced himself to shut up.

"The bargain entails that the mother gives birth at court," Oberon reminded Fosch. "If the scion is male, both mother and infant can return home." Oberon then would need to take other measures, but he too, was aware of the ultrasound's results.

"That's only if she were human," Fosch replied.

Just then, Bella came into the living room, her brown hair mussed from sleep, her foot bare, her aura as blue as a human's. Her eyes, more green than hazel today, were sharp as she focused on Oberon with the intensity of a laser beam.

"I know you," she said. "I see you in my dreams." She cocked her head. "Oberon, the Seelie consort."

"And you are?" Oberon asked, hiding his surprise.

Maybe the charmer hadn't been as thorough as she'd claimed to be.

"Bella."

"And your mother?"

Bella frowned and glanced at Fosch. Doubt began showing in her eyes, the dawning of a primeval fear.

"With all due respect," she said, "I don't see how that's your concern."

"It is, indeed. Who sired you?"

Again, Bella glanced at Fosch, and her panic tore at him. He growled at Oberon, something he never thought himself capable. Not the growling part, but the urge to protect that came over him. It was in that instant he realized Bella was his mate.

Oberon stilled, moving his gaze from Bella to Fosch, back and forth. Fosch placed an arm around Bella's shoulder, her enormous belly rippling with the scion's movement.

Mine. He growled again and glared at Oberon, his eyes flashing yellow with his inner beast.

"You will respect my mate."

The words shocked them all, even Fosch.

Oberon recovered first. "You have mated a human, Dhiultadh Yoncey Fosch."

"She. Is. Not. Human," Fosch gritted.

Beside him, Bella's shoulders jerked, and a crease appeared between her brows. Oberon turned to Bella, who recoiled into Fosch's side, who growled in return.

"Who sired you?" Oberon demanded.

Fosch wanted to rip into Oberon, but reason began to creep in. He forced himself to take a deep breath, realizing Oberon wouldn't give up without verifying for himself.

Fosch pushed Bella back a few inches so he could look into her frightened eyes.

"It's okay. This is just a misunderstanding. Go ahead and tell him."

Bella shook her head, her hair bouncing wildly, her gaze darting everywhere. Fosch put a warm hand on her cheek, conscious of Oberon's watchful eyes, and forced Bella to look at him.

"Hon, I promise you it's okay. All you need to tell him is who your parents were so he can verify for himself that you're not who he thinks you are."

Bella's lips moved, but no words came out.

"Louder, hon. Come on, you can do this." Fosch massaged the knots on her shoulder with one hand and kept his other over her cheek.

Bella's lips trembled and parted. Her gaze darted sideways. "I-I-I can't remember."

It took Fosch a few seconds to comprehend her words. For a moment, he didn't move. Then with a ferocious roar that shook the house, he jumped on Oberon, sharp teeth and talons bared, only to freeze an inch before Oberon's throat.

"To attack Seelie royalty," Lee said smoothly, "is to forfeit your life, Dhiultadh Yoncey Fosch."

"He did something to my mate," Fosch spat, his teeth too large to be accommodated by his still human mouth.

"I did not," Oberon replied calmly.

Fosch narrowed his eyes, for he knew the Seelie couldn't lie, but were well-crafted in the art of evasion.

"You sent someone."

"I did not."

"You did something to my mate to make her human."

Here Oberon tread carefully. "I have no part, Dhiultadh Fosch, by any means, foul or otherwise, in the happenstance of your mate being human today."

Fosch glared at Oberon. "Neither directly or indirectly?"

Oberon met his stare. "I am not responsible, directly or indirectly, for the status of your mate's mortality, Dhiultadh Fosch. Neither are my people, directly or indirectly. If she is human, it is because that's what she is. It is through no doing of mine."

Fosch deflated, and returned his talons to fingers and his teeth back to normal. He took a step back and Leon lowered the dagger she had poised at his throat. Fosch turned and looked at Bella, still standing where she had been when he'd jumped Oberon, frozen, eyes wild, skin pale.

"She is human," Leon said beside Oberon. "Completely so."

Fosch growled, but he didn't look at them. Instead, he kept his gaze fixed on Bella, at the way her shoulders trembled, her stomach rippled, hands fisted beside her. He tilted his head, studying her plain blue aura. Not a flicker of the witchy sheen was present now. She jerked again, her eyes widened, her skin paled even more.

Fosch's nostrils flared. "What—"

Bella fainted. Her eyes rolled back, the whites showing,

and she went limp. Fosch caught her before she could hit the ground, and lowered her gently to the floor.

"Bella?" he choked. "Bella? Bella? Please say something."

Leon crouched beside him and studied the prone woman without touching her.

"The scion is coming," she announced in her cold voice.

❦ 10 ❦

THE OUTCOME

At the hospital, Fosch paced back and forth. He wanted to take her to someone with more experience with the preternatural world, but there wasn't any time, even if skipping through the leeway were possible in her condition. She was too weak for that, and he had no idea where the clan's healer was.

There was internal hemorrhaging, the doctor had said before ushering Bella to an operating room, and at the moment, like it or not, she was human. Fosch clenched his jaws, felt a welcoming ache, clenched his fists. He spun around when Oberon entered the waiting room.

"What are you doing here?" Fosch demanded, almost feral now.

Oberon stared into Fosch's eyes, flashing black and yellow, and crossed his arms.

"I have Benty watching over the procedure. She will report soon."

Fosch felt the fight abandon him, and his knees weaken.

"A Seelie healer would make the process easier,"

Oberon said, tone conversational. "I took the liberty to send for Hiendrich."

Hiendrich, the best healer in the entire Sidhe land. A powerful Seelie, considered only one step below Queen Titania.

No, no...

But Fosch didn't voice the protest. He'd give anything right now for his mate's safety, including an open favor to his enemy. Oberon watched him fight with himself. Watched as Fosch's eyes flashed yellow, once, twice. Under any other circumstances, he would have never interfered, but this was an emergency, one Oberon cared greatly about its outcome.

Oberon stiffened and turned around to face the door.

"What? What?" Fosch jumped beside him, grabbed him by the arm and whirled him around. "Tell me!"

Oberon snarled at him, and for the first time, Fosch saw anger darken the expression of the Seelie consort–and couldn't care less. Benty popped into existence in front of Oberon, just as Fosch was about to shake him. The pixie spoke agitatedly, in the high-pitched tone that Fosch couldn't understand. He had an urge to pluck the pixie out of the air and start squeezing it for information, so Fosch fisted his hands.

Oberon listened, then looked at Fosch, his expression blank. Benty popped away, disappearing just as a doctor, white-faced and eyes wild, turned into the room. There was blood on his green scrubs and gloves. Fosch was pretty sure that wasn't supposed to be there. Not when the doctor came to visit an expecting father to deliver the good news.

"Sir... Sir... the baby..."

The doctor swallowed. Fosch recognized hysteria in the man's voice and took a step forward.

"Sir... she's got..." The doctor swallowed once, twice.

"Talons," he whispered, his crazed eyes rolling back before he fainted.

Fosch didn't try to catch him. The man's nose smacked the tile floor, and blood began oozing from his nose and busted lips. With a calmness he didn't feel, Fosch stepped over the prone doctor and moved toward the operating room, toward the hysterical screams he knew came from Bella's room.

Fosch stood in the middle of the stone circle, surrounded by his kin and Seelie. To his right stood his people, the Council of the Unseelie Dhiultadh in the middle. To his left the Seelie courtiers, with Queen Titania and Oberon in the front and slightly apart. Fosch had witnessed this type of execution only once, though they had been common during his grandfather's reign.

"Dhiultadh Yoncey Fosch," Leon said, "you have made a bargain with the Seelie consort, Oberon. Do you deny?"

"I do not."

"This bargain entails a human hybrid, the offspring of a human female, and you. Do you deny?"

"I do not."

Leon turned around to face the crowd. "We have gathered today to witness the execution of Dhiultadh Yoncey Fosch, son of Dhiultadh Bran Fosch, for denying the Seelie consort his rightful prize."

Oberon slowly stepped forward, relaxed, jeweled sword by his side. He met Fosch's gaze, showed none of the regret he felt.

"Dhiultadh Yoncey Fosch, I hereby give you this one last chance. Do you die like a coward, or do you fulfill our bargain?"

Fosch met Oberon's gaze. "My daughter will not be raised as a Seelie whore."

Oberon stepped back and inclined his head one last time. "Do you confirm that you forfeit your own life, Dhiultadh Yoncey Fosch?"

"I do," Fosch replied, calmly.

He refused to look when Archer murmured his protest.

"Let it be known," Leon called above the murmuring Fee and Dhiultadh, "that Dhiultadh Fosch has been given one more chance to repent and has refused."

Fosch glanced at Oberon, found no traces of triumph or mockery in the Seelie's face. On the contrary, the Seelie consort seemed somber, grim even.

Leon turned to the assembled crowd. "Dhiultadh Fosch has been sentenced to the coward's death, by the claws of the Jubada, and we all bear witness today."

He was already dead inside, detached from the man he had been once. Like an empty shell. The only reason he'd held on this long was to save his daughter from a horrible fate, to honor his mate's sacrifice.

He had felt his daughter's strength when he held her in the hospital, had helped her retract her tiny talons. He had known from the moment he held her that she would be strong. Her aura, despite looking plain and human, had blazed full of power, and Fosch had performed a ritual of containment to keep his daughter's strength bound until her first shift, which only happened at the cusp of the scion's puberty cycle, and only at the presence of the clan's leader. He trusted his brother to seek help if his daughter exhibited more power than Archer was accustomed to dealing with.

Fosch turned and met Archer's eyes. "My daughter's name is Roxanne."

He looked away before his brother could voice a

denial, and strolled to the pit that had been prepared. He would've rather died by the sword, but for his daughter's sake he accepted the coward's death. In reality, any death would be preferable to a life without his mate. As he knelt, he recalled the joyful times he had spent with her.

Fosch closed his eyes, but not before he saw Oberon clench his fists, and Queen Titania tighten her jaws. He heard the galloping hooves of the Jubada approaching, heard Bella's laughter, recalled his daughter's dark eyes looking up at him, and he knew she was destined for a great future.

EPILOGUE

All seven members of the High Council of the Unseelie Dhiultadh assembled in the green room and watched the infant sleep. They had gathered to decide the hybrid's future, to agree upon her fate.

"It's an abomination," Alleena said, indignant merely to be in its presence.

"I still can't believe he gave his life for her," Ruben murmured, the grief apparent in his dark eyes.

The youngest in the group, he was, without knowing, the only one who felt sympathy for the scion.

"What kind of bargain could he have possibly made?" Jaspion asked.

They all looked at Archer, but he didn't answer. His shock didn't show through his passive facade, one he had learned through mimicking his older brother. He had learned plenty from him. Had adored him as a child, looked for approval as a youngling, and had asked for counseling as a man. Even when Fosch had passed leadership on to him, it was to Fosch he turned to when a challenge had been issued, a problem had been presented.

The news of the execution had shocked Archer, so much that he had refused to believe the truth until he arrived at the stone circle and watched his brother refuse to fulfill the bargain.

Archer recalled that year in the spring when he had miraculously recovered from the plague, the vague memory of waking up in the middle of the night to find his brother standing by his bed, his eyes glowing orange with his Earth witch power. Fosch had known he'd been infected, and had sent Arianna after Zantry so they could help him, or kill him if they couldn't–to spare his brother the heartache of having to do it himself.

Archer touched his forehead, the place where a scar once marked his skin for a few hours, scrubbed his index finger over the phantom mark.

"We could leave her in the wilderness," Bebbette suggested from his right.

The oldest in the group, she was the one who still clung to old traditions and rules with teeth and claws. She hadn't liked when Fosch had passed leadership over to Archer. Had even challenged Archer for a dual. He won the challenge, and against Fosch's caution, let her live—a respect he bestowed to his elder. Although she hadn't thanked him then, she'd long since come around and become one of his trusted friends.

"Or send her for Cora to raise," Thalia said.

She was one of the few who remembered to pass on the news to Cora, Fosch's younger sister, leader of the Earth Witch Coven.

"Or outright kill her," said Saydy, Thalia's mate. "She's so tiny. She won't put up a fight."

They sniggered in unison.

"Enough!" Archer snapped. "We aren't going to kill

her. We aren't going through all that hassle with the human court to just get rid of her."

"What do you suggest?" Alleena asked. "Are you going to raise her on your own?" She smirked. "You already have one incompetent mixed breed. It wouldn't be any hardship on you to downgrade to a human hybrid."

In truth, Alleena felt entitled to Logan's position, believed she had been robbed from it since she was Fosch's stepsister and older than Archer by a few years. Now, this hybrid appeared out of nowhere and Alleena felt threatened by it.

Archer cocked his head and met Alleena's unflinching stare. He knew she coveted Logan's position, but rules dictated that he was given enough time to heal after the death of a mate. And for Arianna, Archer would give Logan, the son of Arianna's heart, as much time as he needed.

"That incompetent mixed breed you mock, Alleena, is my second, the mate of my daughter. I will be sure once he has recovered from the shock of losing his mate, to make you the first to challenge him if you so wish. Unless you'd rather challenge me?"

Alleena looked away, as Archer knew she would. Logan was the best fighter he had, no matter if he wasn't a pure blood. He was a mix between the two Dhiultadh clans, both his parents turned rogue and deceased.

Archer looked around at the six faces surrounding him, met everyone's gaze until each looked away.

"Her name is Roxanne," he said. "You will call her by name, Roxanne Fosch." He read the defiance in everyone's eyes. "I don't know why the bargain was struck, except that Fosch would've had a damn good reason for it. All of you have admired my brother for his cunning, followed his leadership for centuries without a doubt. One deed that we don't even know the reason for, and every one of you is thinking poorly of him. Which one of you has never committed a wrong, something to be ashamed of?"

This time, there was shame on a few faces before they turned away.

"Now, I'm not going to throw his sacrifice away without knowing why he did what he did." He inclined his head at the smirking Alleena. "You will raise her and discover why."

Alleena's smirk faded. He waited for her to swallow her denial and rephrase it again. "And if there's nothing to find?"

"The government wants her for research. You will pick up the fight in court for her as her mother's only living relative." Archer raised his voice to cut off Alleena's protest. "And as the clan's only scientist, you will study the child's blood as she grows."

Alleena snapped her mouth shut, her eyes blazing with anger.

"And if there's more to her?" Ruben asked. "Fosch had been acting recklessly—"

He ignored Archer's warning growl and continued, "But I know for a fact he was a smart man, probably had a good reason to do what he did. Maybe there's something we're missing."

Archer inclined his head. "If there is something, Roxanne will disappear before we have to fulfill the human's verdict."

"And if there's nothing to find?" Alleena repeated.

Archer looked at the infant, contemplated the small bundle, remembered his own daughter. His heart iced, hardening against the emotion that tried to well up.

"If there's nothing, we can use her to make the humans lose interest in catching one of us."

There was a flicker of guilt inside him, dulled by the inner numbness resulted by all he had lost. And as the other members of the council looked at one another, Archer wondered if he'd regret this decision one day.

There was a shocked pause before Jaspion chuckled. "Ah, if they find that she's no more than a lesser preternatural, then there's no reason for their persistence."

Bebbette nodded. "It was Fosch's fault they got on our trail in the first place. It's only fair his daughter fixes his mess."

Decision reached, everyone stood and left the council room, except for Archer and Roxanne. At the door, Ruben paused and turned back.

"Sir, I'm sorry for your loss," He said and left.

Archer recalled all he had lost these past years. A daughter, a lover, a friend, and now a brother.

He frowned down at his brother's daughter, hoped she would prove to be more than she looked, for his brother's sacrifice. Then he called Laura, his in-house assistant, and ordered her to take the hybrid upstairs, to the room across from Logan's.

THE END

Dear reader,

We hope you enjoyed reading *The Curse*. Please take a moment to leave a review, even if it's a short one. Your opinion is important to us.

Discover more books by Jina S. Bazzar at https://www.nextchapter.pub/authors/jina-s-bazzar

Want to know when one of our books is free or discounted? Join the newsletter at http://eepurl.com/bqqB3H

Best regards,

Jina S. Bazzar and the Next Chapter Team

ABOUT THE AUTHOR

Jina S. Bazzar is a freelance writer, a blogger, and a mother. She was born and raised in Brazil, and currently lives in the middle-east. She led a normal, uneventful life until she developed a chronic disease during her late teens that caused her to go blind.

To find out more about her writing, her daily life and funny mishaps, visit her on her page:
   www.authorsinspirations.wordpress.com

You might also like:

Heir of Ashes by Jina S. Bazzar

To read the first chapter for free, head to:
https://www.nextchapter.pub/books/heir-of-ashes

Lightning Source UK Ltd.
Milton Keynes UK
UKHW022311021120
372685UK00003B/493

9 781715 742003